THE SHAPING AND RESHAPING OF EARTH'S SURFACE™

Minerals
and the Rock Cycle

Joanne Mattern

The Rosen Publishing Group's
PowerKids Press™
New York

Published in 2006 by The Rosen Publishing Group, Inc.
29 East 21st Street, New York, NY 10010

First Edition

Editor: Melissa Acevedo
Book Design: Ginny Chu

Illustrations: Pp. 6 and 7 by Ginny Chu.
Photo Credits: Cover and title page, pp. 4 (bottom), 15 (gypsum, calcite, apatite, orthoclase, topaz), 17 © José Manuel Sanchis Calvete/Corbis; pp. 4 (top left) © Jonathan Blair/Corbis; pp. 4 (top right), 13 (bottom), 15 (fluorite) © Maurice Nimmo; Frank Lane Picture Agency/Corbis; p. 8 © Anthony Bannister;Gallo Images/Corbis; p. 9 (left) © Arne Hodalic/Corbis; p. 9 (right) © M. Angelo/Corbis; p. 10 © Royalty-Free/Corbis; p. 11 © Lowell Georgia/Corbis; p. 12 © Carl & Ann Purcell/Corbis; p. 13 (top left and right) Christian Thorsten; pp. 14, 15 (diamond) © Thom Lang/Corbis; p. 15 (talc) © Dr. Richard Busch; pp. 15 (quartz), 18 (top right) © Layne Kennedy/Corbis; p. 15 (corundum) USGS/Mineral Information Institute; p. 16 Matthias Kulka/Corbis; p. 18 (top left) © James L. Amos/Corbis; p. 18 (bottom) © Christie's Images/Corbis; p. 20 © Darbellay Nathalie/Corbis Sygma; p. 21 © Michael Freeman/Corbis.

Library of Congress Cataloging-in-Publication Data

Mattern, Joanne, 1963–
  Minerals and the rock cycle / Joanne Mattern.— 1st ed.
     p. cm. — (Shaping and reshaping of Earth's surface)
  Includes index.
  ISBN 1-4042-3199-4 (library binding)
  1. Minerals—Juvenile literature. 2. Rocks—Juvenile literature. I. Title.

  QE365.2.M38 2006
  549—dc22
                              2005003724

Manufactured in the United States of America

Contents

The mineral potassium feldspar usually has streaks.

The mineral mica is so soft a fingernail can scratch it.

There are about eight common minerals found on Earth. They are quartz, potassium feldspar, plagioclase feldspar, olivine, pyroxene, amphibole, mica, and calcite. Scientists know of more than 4,000 different minerals.

Right:
This is the mineral calcite. Most seashells are made from it.

Minerals

What Are Minerals?

All rocks are made of natural nonliving solid substances called minerals. Minerals are formed from elements like oxygen and sodium. Elements are the simplest substance that can exist. A specific mineral is always made up of the same elements, no matter what kind of rock it forms.

Some rocks, like limestone, are made of only one mineral. Other rocks have more minerals. This is because heat or pressure forced many different minerals together to create the rock. Most rocks have between 2 and 10 minerals.

All rocks are made of natural nonliving solid substances called minerals. Minerals are formed from elements like oxygen and sodium.

Minerals in the Rock Cycle

Because minerals form all rocks, they are an important part of the rock cycle. The rock cycle is the process by which rocks are broken down to create new rocks. This cycle has been shaping Earth's surface for millions of years.

The rock cycle starts when hot magma rises to the surface of Earth. Once on the surface, it cools and hardens into igneous rocks. Igneous rocks have minerals in the form of tiny crystals. Over time these rocks and their minerals are worn down to form sedimentary rocks. Another type of rock, metamorphic rock, is formed when heat and

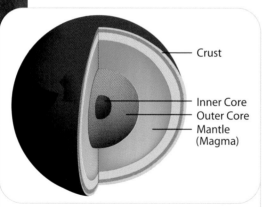

— Crust

— Inner Core
— Outer Core
— Mantle
(Magma)

Earth is made up of several different layers. The top layer of Earth is made of rock and is called the crust. Underneath the crust is the mantle, which is a layer of hot liquid magma. Deep inside Earth are the outer and inner cores. The inner core is a solid metal ball.

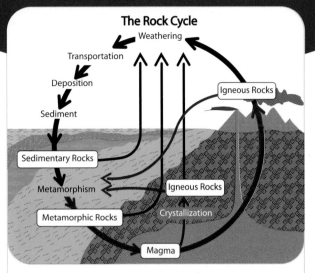

The Rock Cycle

Weathering

Transportation

Deposition

Sediment

Igneous Rocks

Sedimentary Rocks

Metamorphism

Igneous Rocks

Metamorphic Rocks

Crystallization

Magma

This diagram shows the process of the rock cycle. Minerals are included in every step of the rock cycle. They are what creates each of the types of rocks.

pressure change the minerals inside igneous and sedimentary rocks. Sometimes heat and pressure force these minerals together. Other times the heat and pressure add elements to the minerals, which forms new rock. This makes minerals an important part of the rock cycle. As long as minerals keep changing to form new rocks, the rock cycle will go on.

Another type of rock, metamorphic rock, is formed when heat and pressure change the minerals inside igneous and sedimentary rocks.

Building Blocks of Minerals

Native Elements and Compounds

Minerals are made up of substances called elements. Some elements are oxygen, hydrogen, sodium, and gold. Chemical elements, like oxygen, are arranged in a certain way or pattern in a mineral. That arrangement is the mineral's chemical composition. Every mineral has a different chemical composition. It is like the

Quartz is a common mineral compound. It is made of two elements, which are silicon and oxygen.

mineral's fingerprint.

Minerals made of just one element are called native minerals. Some native minerals are made from the elements gold, silver, copper, or mercury. Most minerals are combinations of two or more elements. These minerals are called compounds. Salt is made from two chemical elements, sodium and chlorine.

Olivine is a common mineral. It gets its name because it is the same color as a green olive. Olivine melts when there is a lot of heat. It is one of the first minerals to form crystals when magma cools.

Elements are made of tiny substances called atoms. Atoms are the smallest part of an element. An element's atoms arrange themselves to copy the pattern of the element they are in.

Gold is a native element used to make jewelry.

This picture is a close-up of the mineral copper.

Chemical elements are arranged in certain ways in a mineral. That arrangement is the mineral's chemical composition.

9

Crystal Patterns

The atoms in a mineral are always arranged in a particular pattern. Atoms are able to arrange themselves in these various patterns through a tiny electrical charge they give off. This charge causes some of the atoms to stick together. The atoms that stick together in a mineral are called crystals.

Scientists called geologists study the crystals' patterns to figure out what kind of mineral they are looking at. Crystals come in many different shapes. The mineral halite has crystals that are shaped like cubes. The mineral zircon has

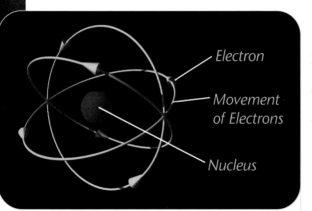

Electron

Movement of Electrons

Nucleus

This is a diagram of an atom. An atom is made up of a nucleus and electrons. The nucleus is the part that holds almost all the atom's mass, or weight. Inside the nucleus are positively charged parts called protons. The electrons are the negatively charged parts of the atom that move around the nucleus to give the atom energy.

crystals that are shaped like two pyramids that are stuck together. Crystals can also have smooth, flat sides, called faces. If you broke a mineral into tiny pieces, every crystal inside each

Water is not a mineral because it is not solid and does not have crystals. However, ice, shown above, is solid and has crystals. Therefore, it is a mineral!

piece would have the same pattern.

Scientists called geologists study the crystals' patterns to figure out what kind of mineral they are looking at. Crystals come in many different shapes.

Properties of Minerals

Physical Properties

All minerals have certain physical properties, which help scientists identify them. One of the most important qualities is hardness. A harder mineral will always scratch a softer mineral. Scientists test hardness by scratching one mineral with another.

Some minerals glow in the dark! This is called fluorescence. Fluorite, franklinite, and willemite are three fluorescent minerals.

After scientists perform this test, they compare the results to a chart called the Mohs' scale.

Color is another physical property. However, a mineral is not always the same color. This occurs because of imperfections in the rock. For this reason color

The mineral opal does not have a shiny luster. It looks like wax.

This is how willemite looks under regular light.

This is how willemite looks as it glows in the dark.

is not the only property scientists use to identify a mineral. They also use the color of a mineral's streak. When you scratch a mineral against a piece of tile, it leaves a streak behind. For example, though the mineral fluorite comes in many colors, such as blue or green, it always leaves a white streak.

This fluorite rock from England glows in the dark. Fluorite is one of three fluorescent minerals.

Luster is another property. It measures how shiny a mineral is. The mineral graphite is very shiny. It looks metallic when you hold it under a light.

All minerals have certain physical properties, which help scientists identify them.

Mohs' Scale

Scientists would not be able to use hardness to identify a mineral if the Mohs' scale did not exist. In 1822, a scientist named Friedrich Mohs invented a scale that shows the hardness of different minerals by scratching them. The Mohs' scale lists how hard 10 common minerals are.

Diamonds are made from the chemical element carbon. Their color varies, although colorless is most popular for jewelry. Diamonds can also be red, blue, black, or yellow.

The scale goes from 1 to 10. The mineral that is listed as number 1 is the softest mineral. The mineral listed as number 10 is the hardest. Talc is number 1 on the Mohs' scale. It is so soft you can scratch it with your fingernail. Diamond is number 10 on the Mohs' scale. Only a diamond can scratch another diamond!

The Mohs' scale does not list every mineral. Instead it lists 10 common minerals that have different levels of hardness. Using the Mohs' scale is a simple and useful way to get an idea of how hard a mineral is.

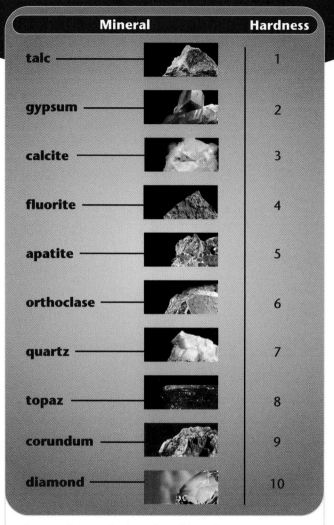

Mineral		Hardness
talc		1
gypsum		2
calcite		3
fluorite		4
apatite		5
orthoclase		6
quartz		7
topaz		8
corundum		9
diamond		10

This is the Mohs' scale of hardness.

The Mohs' scale does not list every mineral. Instead it lists 10 common minerals that have different levels of hardness.

Taste, Odor, and Magnetism

Taste and odor are also physical properties of minerals. You should never lick a mineral to see what it tastes like, though, because some are poisonous. There are, however, minerals that are not poisonous and that have a strong taste. The most common of these minerals is halite. The salt we use on our food is made from halite.

Most minerals do not have a strong smell. That can change if the mineral is heated or struck very hard. The mineral

About 2,800 years ago, people in China saw that one end of a loose rock that had magnetite in it always pointed north. Soldiers and sailors began using magnetite to help them find their way. This is how the compass, shown above, was invented!

16

barite has no odor until it is heated. Then it smells like rotten eggs!

There are a few minerals that are magnetic. These minerals are very easy to identify.

Barite is used in some inks and plastics and as an ingredient in makeup.

Magnetite got its name because it is magnetic. This mineral draws other metals to it. These kinds of physical properties can provide some clues to a mineral's identity.

You should never lick a mineral to see what it tastes like, though, because some are poisonous.

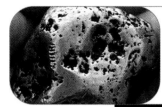

This piece of platinum was found in Russia.

This vein of gold was located in a quartz rock.

One ounce (28 g) of gold can be made into a thin wire that would stretch more than 1 mile (1.6 km) long. One ounce of gold can also be hammered into a thin sheet that covers 100 square feet (9 sq m).

Right:
This Egyptian statue of a cat is made of bronze.

Different Kinds of Minerals

Metals

Some minerals, like gold and platinum, are metals that occur naturally in Earth's crust. Gold can be found in cracks in Earth's crust. These places are called veins. Veins of gold are often pushed to the surface because of pressure within Earth. Pure gold is almost impossible to destroy but is soft enough to be shaped. Platinum, found in mines, is one of the heaviest substances on Earth. It is hard and usually used to make jewelry.

Sometimes metals combine to form compounds called alloys. Copper and zinc combine to form brass. Tin and copper make the alloy bronze.

Pure gold is almost impossible to destroy but is soft enough to be shaped. Platinum, found in mines, is one of the heaviest substances on Earth.

Gems

Gems are minerals that have been cut and polished to create beautiful jewels. Diamonds are one of the most valuable gems. For thousands of years, people have worn diamonds as jewelry. They are valued because of their hardness, luster, and beauty. Only 20 percent of the world's diamonds are used to make jewelry. The rest are used to make cutting tools and other machines.

Quartz is another popular gem. Quartz comes in different colors, like white and pink. When quartz combines

A person who cuts and polishes gems is called a lapidary. Lapidaries often cut flat surfaces, called facets, into a gem. These facets reflect the light and make the gem sparkle.

with iron, it can turn purple. Purple quartz is called amethyst.

Corundum is a mineral that can form many different gems. Pure corundum has no color. Red rubies form when heat and pressure add

When exposed to great amounts of heat, a ruby's color changes from red to green. As the gem cools, the green fades away and it turns back to its original red color.

bits of a mineral called chromium to corundum. The presence of the minerals iron and titanium produces a blue gem, called a sapphire.

When quartz combines with iron, it can turn purple. Purple quartz is called amethyst.

The Importance of Minerals

Minerals are important to people in different ways. Without minerals we would not have salt to put on our food. We also would not have graphite to put in our pencils.

Metals are used to build houses, cars, furniture, and many other things. Copper is one of the most useful metals. Copper is very good at carrying electricity. Copper wires carry electricity through most homes. Iron, lead, aluminum, and other metals are used to make machines and other tools.

Minerals make up all the rocks on Earth. Without minerals there would be no rocks, and the rock cycle would not exist. For this reason minerals are a very important part of shaping and reshaping Earth's surface.

Glossary

alloys (A-loyz) Substances composed of two or more elements.

atoms (A-temz) The smallest parts of elements that can exist either alone or with other elements.

chemical (KEH-mih-kul) Having to do with matter that can be mixed with other matter to cause changes.

composition (kom-puh-ZIH-shun) The way something is arranged.

compounds (KOM-powndz) Two or more things combined.

crystals (KRIS-tulz) In a mineral crystals are the pattern in which atoms are arranged.

igneous rocks (IG-nee-us ROKS) Hot, liquid, underground minerals that have cooled and hardened.

jewelry (JOO-ul-ree) Objects worn for decoration that are made of special metals, such as gold and silver, and prized stones.

magma (MAG-muh) A hot liquid rock underneath Earth's surface.

magnetic (mag-NEH-tik) Having to do with the force that pulls certain objects toward one another.

metamorphic rock (meh-tuh-MOR-fik ROK) Rock that has been changed by heat and heavy weight.

minerals (MIN-rulz) Natural elements that are not animals, plants, or other living things.

physical (FIH-zih-kul) Having to do with natural forces.

pressure (PREH-shur) A force that pushes on something.

properties (PRAH-pur-teez) Features that belong to something.

pyramids (PEER-uh-midz) Shapes that have a square base and triangular sides that meet at the top.

sedimentary rocks (seh-deh-MEN-teh-ree ROKS) Layers of stones, sand, or mud that have been pressed together to form rock.

substances (SUB-stan-siz) Any matter that takes up space.

Index

C
chemical composition, 8
copper, 9, 19, 22
crystals, 6, 10–11

D
diamond(s), 14, 20

G
gold, 8–9, 19

H
halite, 10, 16
hardness, 16
hydrogen, 8

I
igneous rocks, 6
iron, 21–22

M
magma, 6
metamorphic rocks, 6–7
Mohs, Friedrich, 14
Mohs' scale, 12, 14–15

O
oxygen, 5, 8

P
physical properties, 12–17
pressure, 5, 7, 21

Q
quartz, 20–21

S
sedimentary rocks, 6–7
sodium, 5, 9

Web Sites

Due to the changing nature of Internet links, PowerKids Press has developed an online list of Web sites related to the subject of this book. This site is updated regularly. Please use this link to access the list:
www.powerkidslinks.com/sres/mineral/